P9-ECL-501

Dinosaur Planet

ISBN 0-7696-4031-1

50395

9 780769 640310

EAN

Library of Congress Cataloging-in-Publication Data

Orme, David.
    Dinosaur Planet/by David Orme; illustrated by Fabiano Fiorin.
        p.cm.—(Lightning Readers. Confident Reader 3)
    Summary: Tom and Kate take an imaginary trip to a planet full of dinosaurs.
    Includes vocabulary words and discussion questions.
    ISBN 0-7696-4031-1 (pbk.)
    (1. Imagination—Fiction. 2. Dinosaurs—Fiction.) I. Fiorin, Fabiano, ill. II.Title.
    III.Series.

    PZ7.O6338Di 2005
    (E)—dc22   2004060688

School Specialty.
Publishing

Text Copyright © Evans Brothers Ltd. 2004. Illustration Copyright © Fabiano
Fiorin 2004. First published by Evans Brothers Limited, 2A Portman Mansions,
Chiltern Street, London W1U 6NR , United Kingdom. This edition published
under license from Zero to Ten Limited. All rights reserved. Printed in China.
This edition published in 2005 by Gingham Dog Press, an imprint of School
Specialty Publishing, a member of the School Specialty Family.

Send all inquires to:
8720 Orion Place
Columbus, OH 43240-2111

ISBN 0-7696-4031-1

4 5 6 7 8 9 10 EVN 10 09 08 07 06 05

Dinosaur Planet

By David Orme
Illustrated by Fabiano Fiorin

GINGHAM DOG
PRESS

Columbus, Ohio

Tom and Kate liked to pretend.
One day, they were space explorers.

They decided to explore a new planet.
"Look!" yelled Tom.

There were dinosaurs everywhere.
Tom and Kate loved dinosaurs.

They saw large, slow dinosaurs.
These dinosaurs ate plants.

They saw small, quick dinosaurs.
These dinosaurs ate meat.

Some of the dinosaurs had horns.

Some of the dinosaurs had plates on their backs.

In the sky, Tom and Kate
saw flying dinosaurs.

In the lake, they saw dinosaurs
that could swim.

In the forest, Tom and Kate found a nest.
It was full of dinosaur eggs.

The baby dinosaurs were very friendly.

Then, the babies' mother arrived.

"She does not look friendly," said Tom.

"Let's get out of here!"

"Quick, run!" said Kate.

"What a dangerous planet!" said Tom.

Tom and Kate found their spaceship.
They quickly took off.

They landed safely back at home.

But something from Dinosaur Planet came home with them, too!

Challenge Words

dangerous   horns

explore   planet

explorers   spaceship

Think About It!

1. Describe the new world that Tom and Kate discovered.
2. Tom and Kate saw many dinosaurs. Brainstorm a list of the different types of dinosaurs that they saw. Which dinosaurs swam in the water? Which dinosaurs flew in the sky?
3. What did Tom and Kate find in the forest?
4. Why did Tom and Kate run back to their spaceship?

The Story and You

1. What did Tom and Kate bring home with them at the end of the story? Do you think this could really happen?
2. If you were Tom or Kate, what would you have done when you saw the mother dinosaur?
3. What do you think life would be like if dinosaurs still roamed the earth?